Franny K. Stein

MAD SCIENTIST

Attack of the 50-Ft. Cupid

READ ALL OF FRANNY'S ADVENTURES

Lunch Walks Among Us
Attack of the 50-Ft. Cupid
The Invisible Fran
The Fran That Time Forgot
Frantastic Voyage

Franny K. Stein

MAD SCIENTIST

Attack of the 50-Ft. Cupid

JIM BENTON

ALADDIN PAPERBACKS

NEW YORK   LONDON   TORONTO   SYDNEY

ACKNOWLEDGMENTS

Senior Editor: Kevin Lewis
Art Director: Dan Potash
Managing Editor: Dorothy Gribbin
Designer: Lucy Ruth Cummins
Production Manager: Chava Wolin
Editorial Assistant: Joanna Feliz

ALADDIN PAPERBACKS
An imprint of Simon & Schuster Children's Publishing Division
1230 Avenue of the Americas, New York, New York 10020
Copyright © 2004 by Jim Benton
All rights reserved, including the right of reproduction in whole or in part in any form.
ALADDIN PAPERBACKS and colophon are trademarks of Simon & Schuster, Inc..
Also available in a Simon & Schuster Books for Young Readers hardcover edition.
Book design by Dan Potash
The text for this book was set in Captain Kidd.
The illustrations for this book were rendered in pen and ink.
Manufactured in the United States of America
First Aladdin Paperbacks edition January 2005
16 18 20 19 17 15
The Library of Congress has cataloged the hardcover edition as follows:
Benton, James K. / Attack of the 50-foot Cupid / Jim Benton.—1st ed.
p. cm.—(Franny K. Stein, mad scientist ; 2)
Summary: Franny tries to prevent chaos when her new lab assistant, Igor, a dog of many breeds,
accidentally lets loose a giant, fifty-foot, arrow-shooting cupid.
ISBN-13: 978-0-689-86292-2 (hc..)   ISBN-10: 0-689-86292-X (hc.)
[1. Dogs—Fiction. 2. Science—Experiments—Fiction. 3. Valentine's Day—Fiction. 4. Schools—
Fiction. 5. Humorous stories.] I. Title.
PZ7.B447547 At 2004   Fic—dc22   2003018635
ISBN-13: 978-0-689-86296-0 (Aladdin pbk.)   ISBN-10: 0-689-86296-2 (Aladdin pbk.)

For Summer and Griffin

and nieces and nephews Mark, Sean, Brad,
Laura, Tommy, Lauren, Jessi, Robert, Allyson,
Dan, Kristen, Rob, Scott, Evan, Laura, Elissa,
Eric, Brooke, Joe, Mike, Lisa, Ashley, Abbey,
and Tess

CONTENTS

Franny K. Stein
MAD SCIENTIST

Attack of the 50-Ft. Cupid

CHAPTER ONE
FRANNY'S HOUSE

The Stein family lived in a pretty pink house with lovely purple shutters down at the end of Daffodil Street. Everything about the house was bright and cheery. Everything, that is, except the bedroom behind the tiny, round upstairs window.

This was Franny's bedroom, and she loved it more than anyplace else in the whole world, because this was where she came up with some of the most exciting new ideas in mad science.

But, as is often the case for mad scientists, it was impossible to get her friends and family to take her work seriously.

Like when Franny presented her recently perfected Personal Cow to her father.

"Hey, Dad. Have a look at this. I genetically engineered a real cow for the portability that today's baby-on-the-go demands. See? Fresh milk anywhere."

"That's nice, Franny," he said without even looking up from his newspaper.

Or when Franny tried to show off her just-debugged Biggerizer to her little brother, Freddy.

"One blast from this device can make things hundreds of times bigger," Franny declared proudly.

"Can you use it in reverse and make your mouth smaller?" Freddy asked.

Franny answered, "It doesn't have a reverse setting. It only makes things bigger, but that's not a bad idea...." Before she could finish, he leapt on his skateboard and, with one swift push, rocketed out of sight.

Or when Franny called Percy, one of her new friends from school, to announce her new Manifester. "You put a picture of something in front of it, flip the switch, and—*ZAP!*—it creates a real three-dimensional reproduction of it."

"Did you ever put ketchup on corn chips?" Percy asked witlessly.

Franny blinked. "Ketchup on corn chips? Did you hear a single word I said, Percy? The Manifester actually makes *real* things from pictures and pictures from real things. It's total madness."

"I like corn chips," he said, and Franny hung up the phone.

Franny's mom had been watching and she felt bad for Franny.

She might not have chosen to have a mad scientist for a daughter, but that's what Franny was.

And since that's what Franny was, her mom had spent a lot of time trying to learn about mad scientists.

One of the things she learned was this: Mad scientists need assistants to whom they can show their tiny cows, weird devices, and crazy gizmos, assistants who were always excited and who always listened.

CHAPTER TWO

FLEAS AND THANK YOU

One afternoon Franny's mom cautiously poked her head into Franny's room. When poking one's head into a mad scientist's lab, it's always best to do so cautiously.

"Franny, honey, I have somebody I want you to meet."

"I'm kind of busy here, Mom. I'm working on a machine that will make dirty socks smell worse."

"Why would you want that?" Franny's mom asked.

Franny paused, then said, "I guess you wouldn't, Mom. But that's how mad science works."

"Okay, but I just thought you might like to meet your new lab assistant."

"A lab assistant?" Franny said, totally forgetting about the sock experiment. More than anything, she had always wanted her very own lab assistant.

"Well," her mom said, "he's not a *pure* Lab. He's also part poodle, part Chihuahua, part beagle, part spaniel, part shepherd, and part some kind of weasly thing that's not even exactly a dog."

Franny stared blankly at the thing Mom had at the end of a leash.

"But he'll always be interested and excited about your projects, sweetheart, and you can teach him to be your assistant. His name's Igor."

Igor coughed and cocked his head. A few
fleas hopped around in his fur. He could tell
right away that he liked Franny, and he hoped
she liked him in return.

"Oh. It's a dog," Franny said flatly, looking
at Igor like he was half a glass of warm water.
"I thought you meant…"

Franny was all ready to tell her mom to take Igor away, but as she looked into her mother's smiling face she could tell that her mom had really and truly thought that Igor was going to be a big hit.

She couldn't bring herself to let her mom down.

"He's perfect, Mom," Franny lied. "Thanks."

"I just knew you'd love him!" Mom squealed, and handed Franny the leash.

Franny led Igor into her room.

"Sit here," she said. "If I need your assistance with anything, I'll let you know."

Igor sat and tried to smile the friendliest smile that a dog with a mouthful of pointy, craggy teeth could smile.

More than anything, Igor wanted to be a mad scientist's assistant. Especially if that mad scientist was Franny.

CHAPTER THREE

GOOD WHELP IS
HARD TO FIND

Back to work," Franny said. Mad scientists are the hardest-working scientists of all. They do not allow interruptions like Igor to get in the way of progress.

Igor couldn't wait to help.

"Igor! Please don't touch the monsters."
Franny groaned when Igor tried to complete a
creature she had just designed.

"Igor! Hands off the devices." Franny moaned when Igor tried to test her new X-ray projector.

Igor helped Franny combine several extremely dangerous chemicals.

"Igor," she said. "Don't touch the test tubes. Please, just don't touch anything."

CHAPTER FOUR
LIFE'S RUFF

The next morning Igor watched quietly as Franny got ready for school. Before she left, she stopped to shake her finger at him.

"I think we've determined that you're a dog and not a lab assistant. So don't touch anything in this room except your dumb little rubber ball. Understand?"

Igor understood.

He concentrated on not touching anything except his dumb little rubber ball, because more than anything, he just really wanted to help.

CHAPTER FIVE

WHAT COULD BE VERSE?

Franny sat in class listening to her teacher, Miss Shelly.

"Now, remember that we'll be celebrating something special at the end of the week," Miss Shelly said. "You'll need to have valentines ready to share."

Franny raised her hand. "Miss Shelly, what are valentines?"

Miss Shelly never understood how Franny could know so much about weird things but so little about normal things.

Franny felt the same way about Miss Shelly.

The simple truth was that Franny, like most geniuses, studied the things she loved and didn't pay much attention to anything else, including holidays.

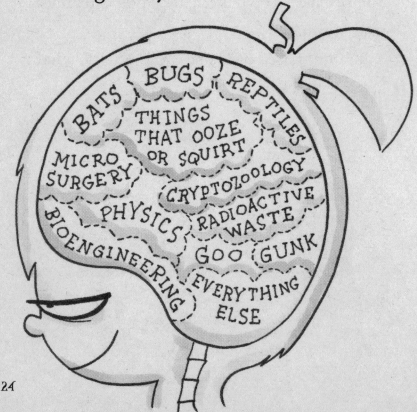

"A valentine is an expression of friendship or love," Miss Shelly began.

"Like for your mom?" Franny asked.

"Well, sure. You can send your mom a valentine. But valentines also celebrate love for those other than your parents."

"I'm not sure I understand," Franny said.

"Here's an example of something you might write on one," Miss Shelly continued. "'Roses are red. Violets are blue. Sugar is sweet, and so are you.'"

"And I write this on every valentine?" Franny asked.

"No, no," said Miss Shelly. "You try to personalize them. You know, express your feelings about the person."

"Okay. You're the boss," Franny said, although she had no idea what Miss Shelly was talking about.

CHAPTER SIX

FRANNY'S VALENTINE~POEM GENERATOR

Later Franny sat at her desk and worked on her assignment.

"I know just the thing to make this much simpler," she said triumphantly. "I'll create one valentine that will work for everyone. That will save a lot of time."

Igor watched quietly, although he really wanted to help.

The next day Franny showed her invention to Miss Shelly.

"It's called the Valentine-Poem Generator. You put the same thing on every valentine, and the recipient just chooses one section from each column. It's called a matrix. This way they can customize it for themselves. There are 625 different combinations."

Franny's Valentine-
Poem Generator

Compose your very own valentine poem. Just take one section from each column and put them together in order.

Roses are red.	Violets are blue.	Sugar is sweet.	And so are you.
Pimples are pinkish.	I play the kazoo.	Turkeys are dumb.	Your family is too.
Boogers are green.	A clog is a shoe.	Bigfoot is hairy.	I believe this is true.
Weasels are brown.	You need a shampoo.	Oatmeal is lumpy	But much less than you.
Zombies are gray.	My toenails regrew.	Diapers are stinky.	This poem is through.

Miss Shelly smiled. She looked at Franny's card and then back at Franny.

"Franny, this is very clever, but maybe I didn't explain it very well. Perhaps adding some decorations or pictures might help."

"Oh, yeah!" Franny said. "Like pictures of the boogers and Bigfoot, right?"

"Well, I was thinking about a picture of something more traditional," Miss Shelly corrected. "Like Cupid."

"Cupid?" Franny asked. "What's that?"

"Well," Miss Shelly explained, "Cupid is this little naked guy with wings. He flies around shooting people with special arrows."

Franny was fascinated. "And people like him?"

"People love him." Miss Shelly laughed. "And sometimes he has little hearts floating around him."

Franny smiled. "Hmm, hearts. Well, I like that part," she said.

"And he's always saying something mushy," Miss Shelly said.

"Mushy," Franny said as she took notes. "And this is all there is to this love stuff?" Franny asked.

Miss Shelly smiled. "Well, there are other things, like flowers and candy, I suppose, but Cupid is a good start, Franny."

CHAPTER SEVEN

DRAWING CONCLUSIONS

Back at home Franny looked over the notes she had made at school.

"Naked. Wings. Arrows," she mumbled. "And hearts."

She looked at her drawing.

"Oh, and he always says something mushy," she whispered. "Let's see—intestines are pretty mushy."

"I have the hang of this valentine thing," Franny said confidently, and she designed a few more, just for good measure.

Igor watched quietly, but he really, really, really wanted to help.

CHAPTER EIGHT

CUPID IS AS
CUPID DOES

Franny couldn't wait to show her new valentines to her friends.

Miss Shelly followed the screams.

"See?" Franny said. "Cupid."

Miss Shelly gasped.

"I had a hard time choosing the mushy thing for him to say, but then I figured that nothing was mushier than guts."

Miss Shelly was speechless.

"Do you want to see the rest?" Franny asked.

Miss Shelly nodded.

Franny's Valentines

VALENTINE, I HOPE YOU ARE PUNCTURED TO A SATISFACTORY DEGREE.

YOU WON'T BE MY VALENTINE?

WELL, SUTURE SELF.

VALENTINE, YOU'RE SUCH A TREASURE.

MAYBE YOU SHOULD BE BURIED.

"Franny," Miss Shelly said finally, "you'd better have a look at this." And she handed Franny a real valentine.

CHAPTER NINE

PINK. CUTE. I'M GOING TO BE SICK.

Franny stared at the card. So *this* was what Miss Shelly was talking about. This was Cupid: all fat, and pink, and adorable.

"Ugh. Now, what is it that this guy does again?" Franny asked.

"He flies around and shoots his little arrows and makes people fall in love."

"Pretty horrible, huh?" Franny said.

Miss Shelly laughed.

Franny looked at her friends. She still didn't understand them, but she was crazy about them. So if a naked baby was what they wanted, that's what they were going to get.

"Okay, Miss Shelly. I understand now," she said, and Miss Shelly lent her the Cupid card to study.

CHAPTER TEN
WORKING LIKE A DOG

Late that night Franny sat at her desk staring at the Cupid card. She still had a lot of work to do if she was going to get cards for everyone done on time, but her heart just wasn't in it.

"I'm tired," she said, and tossed the card aside. "I'll finish the rest tomorrow."

Igor watched quietly, but he really, really, really, really, really, really wanted to help.

After Franny went to bed, Igor tried to sleep. But he was still upset about not being allowed to help. He walked around the room looking at Franny's marvelous experiments in progress and reminded himself not to touch them.

He couldn't think of anything to do, until he noticed, up on Franny's desk, his little rubber ball.

CHAPTER ELEVEN

THAT'S THE WAY THE BALL BOUNCES

Igor knew that he *was* allowed to touch the ball, so he carefully climbed up on the chair and reached for it. He took special care not to touch any of Franny's things.

Suddenly the wheels on the chair shifted, and Igor knocked the ball over the table edge.

The ball bounced twice, then hit the switch on Franny's Manifester.

The Manifester fired a beam directly at the
Cupid card, which caused an itty-bitty, real-life
Cupid to drop out the other side.

And—*zwing! zwizz! zwang!*—tiny arrows flew toward Igor as the tiny Cupid started shooting, which is exactly what Cupid is supposed to do.

Zwing! Zwizz! Zwang!

Igor dodged left and right. He made sure not to touch anything, just as Franny had told him.

Igor avoided jars he could've trapped Cupid
in and a butterfly net he could've caught him
with, because Franny had told him not to touch
anything, and Igor was determined to do just
as Franny had instructed.

Suddenly Igor heard a click and a zap, followed by a loud crunching crack. One of Cupid's arrows had bounced off a button on one of Franny's gizmos.

And that gizmo was the Biggerizer.

CHAPTER TWELVE
HEY MEISTER, WATCH THE KEISTER

A loud CRUNCH woke Franny and she looked up. Way up. Through the hole in the ceiling she saw the moon in the early morning sky. It looked pinker and squishier than it ever had before.

"Pinker? Squishier?"

Wait a second, Franny thought. *That's not the moon. . . .*

That's the biggest baby butt the world has ever seen.

CHAPTER THIRTEEN

THE HOLIDAY IS UPON US

Franny jumped out of bed in a flash. She was standing right behind Igor as Cupid fluttered off like a big, adorable, incredibly dangerous blimp.

"Igor!" Franny said angrily. "Do you have any idea what you've done? I told you not to touch anything and you disobeyed me. Now you have released a monster that I don't know how to stop!"

Franny's eyes flashed with a terrible mad-scientist madness that made Igor wilt.

"You're a *terrible* assistant!" Franny shouted in a voice so angry that she didn't even sound like herself. "And when I get back, you had better be gone, you sad, ugly, good-for-nothing, little dog."

Franny snatched the Biggerizer and raced out the door. Igor sat there, brokenhearted, alone. He wondered where sad, ugly, good-for-nothing, little dogs were supposed to go.

Wherever that place is, Igor thought, *it sure isn't here.*

CHAPTER FOURTEEN

LOVE HURTS

*A*ll morning Franny followed Cupid's trail of destruction.

"He doesn't understand how big he is or how dangerous these huge arrows are!" Franny said. "He has to be stopped before he

skewers somebody!" Cupid, in the distance, was
happily firing his arrows in all directions.

And heading right toward him was a school
bus loaded with kids.

"Oh, no!" Franny yelled. "Cupid is going to love them to pieces."

CHAPTER FIFTEEN
LOVE IS A BATTLEFIELD

Franny arrived on the scene just as the bus driver saw the massive Angel of Love.

Immediately the driver hit the brakes. She tried to go in reverse. But the bus stalled instead.

Cupid noticed the stopped bus and the little kids inside, and he was sure they all wanted to be in love.

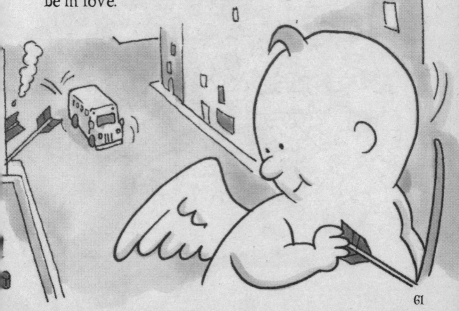

"Think! Think! Think!" Franny said as Cupid nocked an arrow on his bowstring.

The bus driver screamed.

The kids screamed.

Franny wished she had put a reverse button on the Biggerizer. Suddenly she thought of her brother. "Freddy!" she said, and she turned the Biggerizer on herself.

CHAPTER SIXTEEN

THE WHEELS ON THE BUS GO ROUND AND ROUND

Cupid aimed, and—*twang!*—he released a giant arrow, sending it rocketing toward the bus just as Franny came hurtling through the air.

She slammed her right foot on top of the bus and dug her left foot into the dirt as she had seen her brother do countless times.

With a mighty push, Franny was off.

SMASH!

Franny weaved her way through the streets, riding the bus like the biggest skateboard in the world.

Cupid flew after her in hot pursuit, firing arrow after arrow, which Franny ducked and dodged as she tried desperately not to wipe out.

I have to get back to my lab, she thought, and she headed toward Daffodil Street.

CHAPTER SEVENTEEN

MOM ALWAYS SAYS TO WEAR YOUR HELMET

(WHEN YOU BECOME GIGANTIC AND SKATEBOARD ON A SCHOOL BUS)

Franny carved her way around a tight turn and hurtled toward home.

"This skateboarding is kind of fun," she said. "It's not nearly as hard as Freddy says it..."

Franny bounced a wheel off the curb, breaking an axle and sending Franny flying.

"... iiiiiiiiiiiiiis!" she yelled as she tumbled through the air and landed on her front lawn with a very painful crash.

Cupid landed at the end of Daffodil Street
and stomped toward the stopped bus. He had an
arrow all ready to go.

This looked like the end.

Franny's head was spinning. She dragged herself in front of the bus and glowered defiantly.

Cupid pulled back on the arrow and again took aim...

... just as a mouthful of craggy, pointy teeth sank into his giant, squishy butt.

Cupid howled and jumped, and the arrow intended for Franny missed her by an inch.

As Cupid spun around, Franny saw Igor dangling from Cupid's sore pink rump.

Igor had saved her. He had saved the kids on the bus.

Cupid snatched Igor off his butt and threw him to the ground.

He was about to return his attention to Franny when he got a good look at Igor.

Igor was ugly. He was small and pitiful. But more than anything, Cupid could sense that Igor was heartbroken.

And broken hearts were something of *great* interest to Cupid.

"Good. Cupid's distracted." Franny groaned.
"Now we can get out of here!" She started to
limp away, slowly dragging the bus with her.

Cupid held Igor down with his big, fat, pink foot and stared at him. *This*, thought Cupid, *is the brokenest broken heart I have ever seen.*

This called for an extra-big arrow. Cupid reached for the biggest one he had.

CHAPTER EIGHTEEN

NO P.E. NOT TACOS.

Franny hadn't taken more than three feeble steps before she stopped. She remembered when Igor helped with the monster. *That actually was pretty funny*, she thought.

She remembered when he helped with her X-ray projector. *Also pretty funny.*

She remembered how he had risked his life to save her.

She let go of the bus. She was overwhelmed by a strange and powerful electrical charge crackling through her body.

A side effect of the Biggerizer? An injury to her nervous system sustained in the bus wipeout? Yesterday's cafeteria tacos not sitting so well?

Franny felt strangely empowered. She felt strong, and focused.

This wasn't high voltage. This wasn't a chemical reaction. This wasn't a supernatural phenomenon.

She looked at Igor.

"Egads," Franny whispered, and her heart melted.

CHAPTER NINETEEN

IT'S MAD SCIENCE TIME

"Must save Igor" was all Franny could say. But how? Franny's massive brain ran calculations and scenarios at a blurring speed.

Franny knew she could never take Cupid in a fight. He had that bow and arrow. And besides, it wouldn't be right to clobber a baby, even a fifty-foot one. A baby's a baby, right?

As Cupid put the arrow in the bow, Igor looked over at Franny.

"A baby's a baby!" Franny exclaimed. "He might be a gigantic, destructive, arrow-slinging Cupid, but he's still a baby!"

Franny pulled the roof off her house and tore through her beloved laboratory. "Where are you? Where are you?!" she yelled.

Finally she stopped.

"There you are!" she yelled, and fired the Biggerizer.

CHAPTER TWENTY

UDDER MADNESS

Back at the street Igor closed his eyes as hard as he could and waited for the twang of Cupid's arrow.

But he didn't hear a twang.

He heard a splash. Or was it splosh? It was that sort of squirty sound you hear when you turn the garden hose on full blast. Then he heard slurpy sounds and a moo.

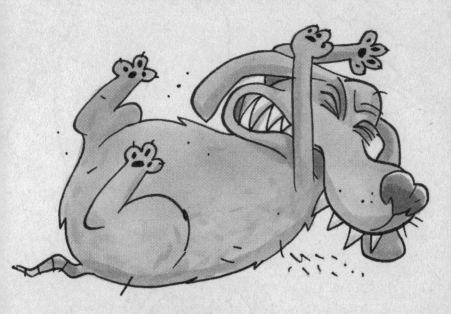

He opened his eyes. Cupid was slobbering up a long stream of some liquid.

And at the other end of the long stream was Franny.

She had used the Biggerizer on the Personal Cow and was squirting an irresistible gush of fresh milk. Cupid had dropped his bow and arrow and was following it like the big, chubby baby he was.

Franny maneuvered him to a spot where she could get a clean shot at him.

And while Cupid busied himself with the cow, Franny activated the Manifester in reverse. With one blast, she returned him to his proper form as the Cupid in a valentine card.

CHAPTER TWENTY-ONE

LGMS SEEKS ULD

(LITTLE GIRL MAD SCIENTIST SEEKS UGLY LITTLE DOG)

Franny stood in her yard. Cupid was no longer a threat and the kids were safe, but strewn on the lawn around her was the smoldering wreckage of her lab.

She should have been the saddest little mad scientist ever.

But she wasn't. She was happy. In fact, she
was very happy.

Igor was okay, and as smart as Franny was,
she would never ever be able to explain why, at
that moment, that was the most important thing.

She stooped down and picked him up. He
looked frightened and sad.

"Um, thanks for saving my life," she mumbled.

Igor trembled. He looked as though he would cry.

"You know," she said, "we mad scientists are sort of excitable. And, uh, sometimes we say things that we don't really mean."

Igor blinked. His eyes widened a bit.

"And really, this is all mostly my fault. I'm the one that made the Manifester and the Biggerizer in the first place."

Igor smiled a little.

"I guess what I'm trying to say is that I'm going to need an assistant to help me get back to normal size and also help put this lab back together.

"And, uh, I was thinking that I'd like you to be my assistant, if you want to. I'd really like it."

Franny felt that strange rush of electricity surge through her again. There was something about revealing how she felt that was almost as powerful as feeling it.

And, incredibly, it seemed to have an effect on Igor.

He sat up straighter. He somehow looked less ugly. His breath got better, and as he wagged his tail happily, dozens of fleas and ticks jumped off his back. They must have realized that Igor was no longer the type of dog that they could infest.

"You're going to be the best lab assistant in the world," Franny said.

Igor jumped from her hand and immediately started to help clean up the yard.

He knocked a flask into a beaker, which blew up, leaving a twelve-foot-wide crater in the yard.

"Okay," Franny said. "Maybe not the best.

"But you'll be MY lab assistant."

CHAPTER TWENTY-TWO
IT MUTTS BE LOVE

Franny and Igor worked together as if they had known each other forever.

They fixed the bus and got the kids off to school.

They built a device to shrink Franny back to normal size.

Along the way they learned that Igor could help a lot by holding things that Franny's giant hands would have probably broken.

And then they made all the Valentine's Day cards that Franny needed to give to Miss Shelly and her classmates.

"This thing is just too dangerous," Franny said, and together they destroyed the Biggerizer.

But not before they used it just one more time.

CHAPTER TWENTY-THREE

AND THAT'S THAT

Miss Shelly and the kids looked out the window. It looked like a giant brown mountain had suddenly appeared in front of the school.

"Happy Valentine's Day," Franny said as she walked in. She handed her cards to Miss Shelly and the kids.

"Franny!" Miss Shelly said. "Are you responsible for that, that *thing* out there?"

"I am," Franny said. "Happy Valentine's Day. It's for you."

"For me?" Miss Shelly said. "Really, Franny, I don't know what that thing is, but I'm quite sure I don't want it."

"Suit yourself," Franny said smiling. "But it's not a 'thing.'

"It's a chocolate-covered cherry."
Miss Shelly gasped.
"You said something about candy."
Miss Shelly and the kids went outside for a
closer look, and Miss Shelly let them dig in.

"It looks like you were hit with one of Cupid's arrows," Miss Shelly said with a happy wink as she enjoyed a taste of the candy.

"I thought so too," Franny said seriously, "but after a complete examination, I found that I wasn't even nicked.

"No, Miss Shelly, there's something strange at work here, a phenomenon I just can't explain. It could take me months to unravel this."

"Months," Miss Shelly said, and she watched as Franny, Igor, and the kids slurped up the giant chocolate-covered cherry.

She opened the envelope that Franny had given her and looked at the card inside.

Miss Shelly—
He's the scariest thing in the world, but I know you like him, so, here's your CUPID—

Love
franny

And Miss Shelly felt that same strange surge of power that Franny had felt crackle through her from head to toe.

"Happy Valentine's Day, Franny," she whispered.